FOLD ME A POEM

KRISTINE O'CONNELL GEORGE

Illustrated by LAUREN STRINGER

Harcourt, Inc.

Orlando   Austin   New York   San Diego   Toronto   London

Requests for permission to make copies of any part of the work should be
mailed to the following address: Permissions Department, Harcourt, Inc.,
6277 Sea Harbor Drive, Orlando, Florida 32887-6777.

www.HarcourtBooks.com

Library of Congress Cataloging-in-Publication Data
George, Kristine O'Connell.
Fold me a poem/Kristine O'Connell George; illustrated by Lauren Stringer.
p. cm.
Summary: A collection of poems about origami animals.
1. Origami—Juvenile poetry.   2. Animals—Juvenile poetry.
3. Children's poetry, American.   [1. Origami—Poetry.   2. Animals—Poetry.
3. American poetry.]   I. Stringer, Lauren, ill.   II. Title.
PS3557.E488F65 2005
811'.54—dc22   2003019382
ISBN 0-15-202501-4

First edition
A C E G H F D B

Printed in Singapore

The illustrations in this book were done in Lascaux acrylics
on Fabriano 140-lb. watercolor paper.
The display type was set in Post Antiqua.
The text type was set in Requiem.
Color separations by Bright Arts Ltd., Hong Kong
Printed and bound by Tien Wah Press, Singapore
This book was printed on totally chlorine-free Stora Enso Matte paper.
Production supervision by Pascha Gerlinger
Designed by Lauren Stringer and Lydia D'moch

For Dustin
—K. O. G.

For Debra Frasier,
who knows the art
of bringing paper to life
—L. S.

Origami

Square sheet of paper—
folded, suddenly wakes up.
Good morning, Rooster.

Buffalo

Crease the shaggy head,
shape the shaggy flanks,
fold sharp horns.

Buffalo
paws the tablecloth.

Buffalo!

Camel

What went wrong?

Lean against
this sand dune
while I double-check
the directions.

Robin's Invitation

Fold a set of wings
for yourself.
I'll show you
sky.

Green Dog's Surprise

You must have been
up late last night,
folding.

This morning,
when I awoke,
I found
three
new friends.

Shadows

Step out of
those dark shadows,
Crow.
We want to
see you.

Cheetah and Lion

Thank you
for our swift running legs!

When we return,
we will let you know
who won the race.

Possibilities

Forty bright sheets
of colored paper,
a world of animals.
Who will be next?

Pond

My lily pad
will not
need a
flower.

It has
a frog.

Peacocks

Won't the peacocks be pleased
when they spread
their new tails?
All these
perfect
pleats.

Spring

At last,
my tulips
arrive,
wearing
paper crowns.

Snake

Folding a snake?
Need advice?
Be precissssssse.

Rabbit Complains

Unbend my ear!
I can't hear
a word
you are
saying.

Recycled

A rumpled paper bag.
Scissors cut a square.
Fold. Crease. Bend.

Behold—

       elephant.

Protection

At one end
of the table,
the rabbits.

At the other end,
the foxes.

I don't
want
trouble.

Black and White Paper

Stacks of black paper.
Stacks of white paper.

Zebras?
Pandas?
Penguins!

White Paper

My hole puncher
clicks and clicks.
Snowflakes,
snowdrifts.

Wind Storm

Hurry, animals!
Get inside the barn.

My brother
just turned on
the fan.

Ostrich's Injury

I'm so sorry
my cat
attacked.

Glue?
Staple?
Tape?
Band-Aid?

Warning!

Please watch
where you hop,
Kangaroo.

That is a
puddle of
glue.

Dragon

Dragon!
Behave yourself.

Remember:
You are
made of
paper.

Of Course

Of course you're real,
Hippopotamus.
Don't you see
your wide
shadow?

Hungry

All afternoon,
the paper cows
have been eyeing
the green paper.

Oh.
Grass!

Impatient

Yes, Monkey.
You may ride
your donkey.

I just finished
painting
the path.

Finishing

Don't fidget, Leopard.
I need to do
your spots.

Disappointed Moth

Why didn't you
save any butterfly colors
for *me*?

Shining Paper

Delicious crinkle—
slinky pieces of foil
flutter between my fingers.

Who wants wings?

Tub

I hope
these boats
will float.

The shore
is lined
with
passengers.

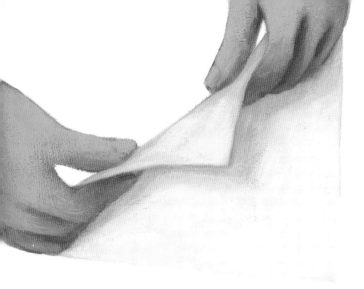

Night

Night
unfolds
softly.

I'll add
my own
star.

Bookmark

Thank you for waiting, Giraffe.
Sit here
by this poem,
and I'll read
to you.

A Song

One last tuck.

Soon
my cricket
will chirp.

Mystery

Before I sleep,
I hear rustling—
soft
papery
whisper-thumps.

Is someone
dancing?

A Note from the Illustrator

When I began the sketches for this book, the only paper-folding skills I had were those required to fold a letter into thirds to fit into an envelope. So, after a trip to the library where I gathered a pile of books on origami, I sat down at my drawing table and began to teach myself the art of folding paper. It took me a week to learn the difference between a *mountain fold* and a *valley fold* and several months of practice to distinguish between a *squash fold* and a *rabbit-ear fold*. Eventually I taught myself *outside-* and *inside-reverse folds, swivel folds, crimp folds,* and the many other folds necessary to create the animals in these poems. It was fun—but it was sometimes hard! If you would like to learn how to make your own paper animals, here are some books to look for:

- Araki, Chiyo. *Origami Activities for Children.* Boston: Tuttle Publishing, 2002.
- Beech, Rick. *The Origami Handbook: The Classic Art of Paperfolding in Step-by-step Contemporary Projects.* New York: Hermes House, 2002.
- Engel, Peter. *Origami from Angelfish to Zen.* Mineola, NY: Dover Publications, 1994.
- Honda, Isao. *The World of Origami.* Tokyo: Japan Publications Trading Company, 1965.
- Kasahara, Kunihiko. *Origami Made Easy.* Tokyo and New York: Japan Publications, 1973.
- Montroll, John. *Animal Origami for the Enthusiast: Step-by-step Instructions in Over 900 Diagrams.* Mineola, NY: Dover Publications, 1985.
- Montroll, John. *Bringing Origami to Life.* Mineola, NY: Dover Publications, 1999.
- Rojas, Hector. *Origami Animals.* New York: Sterling Publishing, 1993.

Visit www.KristineGeorge.com and www.LaurenStringer.com to learn more about origami and to discover fun paper-folding activities.

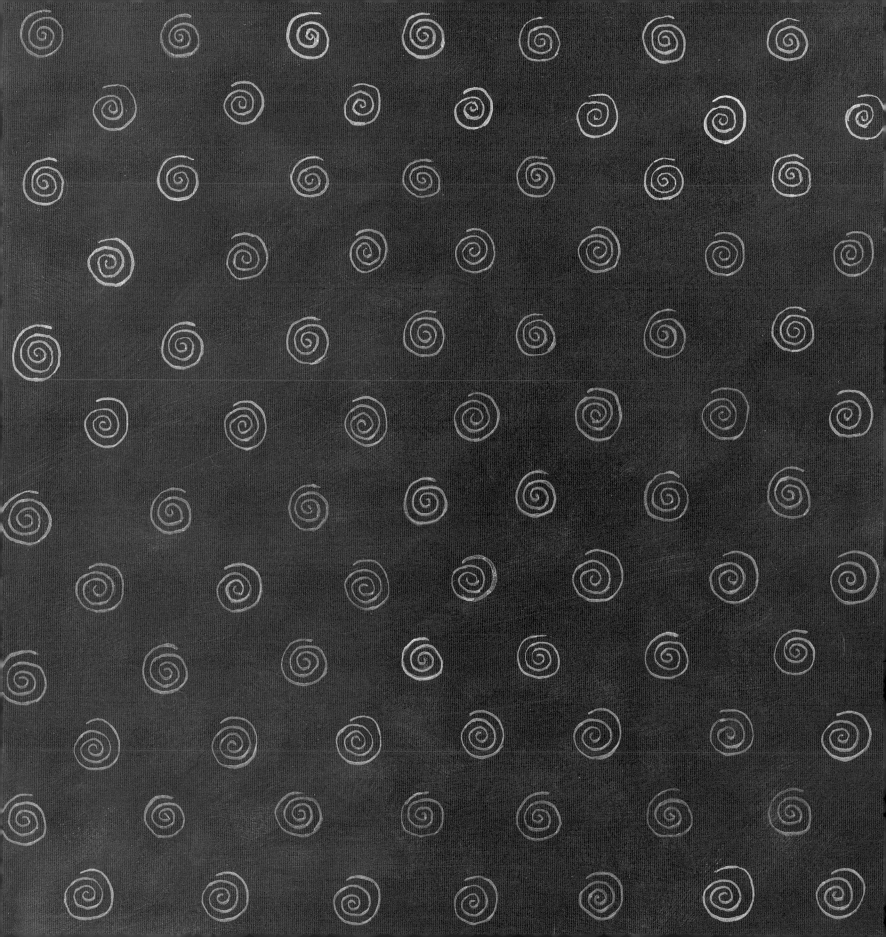